In Their Arms

In Their Arms

by
Thomas Moore

QUEER MOJO
A Rebel Satori Imprint
New Orleans

Book design by Sven Davisson
Cover by Michael Salerno

ISBN 978-1-60864-123-9

This book is dedicated to the following people for their generosity and encouragement when reading the various early drafts of this novel: Michael Salerno, Dave Hilliard, Rebecca Dyer, Kim Davies and Steven Purtill. Thank you so much.

1

The world is full of warmth...

Six hours later I'm asleep in the darkroom. I wake up when the light turns on. The barman tells me to leave. I push against the damp floor and manage to sit up. I struggle to get my jeans and belt to fasten. The barman pulls at my arm and tells me to get out again but angrier than the first time. He only works here because he has to.

The journey home is a blank. I'm so blurry that the world and my interactions with it are too opaque for either component to illuminate the other enough to form anything approaching sense.

There's no music vague enough to fit the mood that I wake up in. I opt for silence. I'd managed to make it on to the bed, which for an optimist could just about be conceived as a plus. I let the tap run and listen to the sound while I reach under the sink for a glass. I let the water overflow quickly and run onto my hands. Water sprays off around the bowl and leaves an imprint on my t-shirt.

There's an ache behind my eyes, like tiredness has swollen and become something solid and tangible. I try to rearrange my thoughts into something linear tracing back through the night. I remember getting to the bar. I remember walking around the darkroom to get an idea of who was there. I remember having to train my eyes to the darkness so I could get used to the movements of shadows, knowing when to avoid old men who are only in a queer place because their wives have died and they're able to clearly differentiate a libido amidst their loneliness. I remember smoking out the back and

1

trying to make the right kind of glance at the people who interested me or I felt I could potentially interest.

It could all be a guess. It could be memories from anywhere.

The buzz of the iPhone on the table feels like a sudden attack. I flinch. A photograph of my friend wearing sunglasses, giving a drunken thumbs-up. I silence the call and flop backwards onto the bed. My jeans are still wet. Sticky denim uncomfortably pulling my leg hairs. I pick up the phone. My friend's face has disappeared and she's relegated to a banner alongside two more missed calls.

Two minutes later and another buzz, another flinch. The water ripples in the glass. A text message: *Hey stranger … are you alive? I guess we could make it dinner if you're not around for lunch?*

When I get my jeans off I realise that there is a hole torn in my underwear, a flap of material hanging out of place.

I run a bath and start to swill mouthwash around my tongue and gums. The inside of my cheeks sting as I inflate them. I let the mouth wash linger long enough to start hurting. I spit it out and lick the roof of my mouth. My tongue doesn't taste as bad as when I woke up.

The bath takes a while to fill. I turn on the coffee machine that I inherited when someone at work got divorced. I make an espresso and drink it quickly from a normal sized mug.

I get into the bath and try to stretch. My neck and back feel sore and I wonder what a massage would feel like right now. I've only ever had friends do it when I've been high or sleepy. I lift my hips and pick at my asshole. I run the tip of my finger around the rim and then rub it with my thumb, letting the miniscule mix of sperm

2

and dried shit dissipate into the water.

A subtle fog of condensation spreads over the small window and mirror. My skin starts to relax. I put a full stop on trying to remember pieces from last night. It feels irrelevant. It'll only make things more complicated. I imagine what drowning would feel like. For about two seconds I'm close to sleep again.

2

I log on to a cruising website and check my messages, using my iPhone. One guy has requested to see my private photos and another has sent a message giving me access to see his. I decline sharing my two private photographs — both of which are pictures of my face — because from the guy's description, and the fact that he doesn't have any photos of himself on his profile, I know that I won't be meeting him. I click on the link from the guy who is sharing private photos, which leads through to his profile. He describes himself as versatile but mostly top and says that he doesn't have a preference when it comes to age but that he's mainly only into white guys. He has four photos. One is of his torso and cock, taken lying down with his head cut out of the shot, one is a close up picture of just his cock and the other two — the privates which he has unlocked for me to see — are of the guy in a bar, one with a friend whose face has been blurred out and another on his own. I send him a message asking him where he lives, because the location on his profile has been left blank.

I check the listings section of the website. I look at the listing for the bar I went to last night. It says that the last comment on the bar was eight hours ago. It's from someone saying that they are planning on visiting the bar in the next few days while he's in town with work, and he's asking if there's a best time to visit or a particular night of the week that is busier than others. No one has posted anything about last night.

I open a cruising app on my phone, pushing my thumb over the screen to scroll through other guys who are nearby. There's a guy who I always see on the train to work, but who I've never spoken to, on the app or in real life. He's never messaged me, which is enough for me to surmise that he has no interest in me. If he were to send me a message, I would sleep with him. The closest guy on the app is just under one thousand metres away, a few streets from me. I've met him before. I've been round to his place for sex three, maybe four times. He's about seven or eight years younger than me but could pass for more. He's given me different names each time I've met him, so I lose track of what I think his name is. There's something about him that stops me from feeling relaxed; an openness maybe, but that doesn't describe it well at all – I'll try again later. He's always on edge – there's a wildness to him. The green light in the corner of his thumbnail disappears. It says he was online ten minutes ago. I haven't met him for sex in about four months.

I make a coffee and pull a chair up to the cluttered table that doubles as a dining area and a workspace. I scoop together a small pile of magazines and loose papers and put them under the desk. I put my phone down and pull my laptop forward and turn it on. I drink the coffee as my eyes skim emails. I open the messages relating to work. One is from the editor of an arts website who has attached a piece that I had sent him two days ago with a list of required edits and suggestions. The editor says that he likes where my article is going but that it perhaps needs to be more specific about certain things that I hint at, and also he wonders if I was trying to get my text to match the tone of the sculptures that I was reviewing – if this is the case then he says he likes that too but I need to make it more explicit.

There's an email from a friend, reminding me to come to his birthday this weekend. He says that if I can make it I can crash at his place. I look for train tickets, although it's Thursday so the cheaper advance deals are gone. I send a short email saying I'll be there and that I wouldn't miss it.

My phone vibrates with a message from the cruising app. It's from the guy who lives near me who I haven't seen in four months. *Hiya sexy. I need cash. You got thirty you could lend me?* It puts me on edge. That message, added to the coffee and the hangover, make me feel anxious. This is the first time we've spoke since we last fucked.

Hey. Sorry – not got cash but how are you?
KK. He adds a sad face to his message.
I repeat myself. *How are you anyway?*
KK cool thanks you?
Hungover! But I'm ok thanks.
You want to fuck me?

I get this shot of fear and suddenly feel sick, but my dick gets hard as I tap a reply. My hands are shaking as I type the message.

Yes.

Maybe because I'm nervous it feels like he's never going to answer me.

I type again. *When?*
Give me fifteen mins?
Cool.

It hits me as almost funny as to how that one tiny word could be such a convincing lie, when I contrast it with just how bad I feel at the moment.

I go to the mirror and wash my face again and run my hand through my hair. I try and find a mint. I change my jeans.

3

He opens his door, smiles and starts to kiss me. He pushes his body onto mine so that we're up against the wall. He's whispering things, which I can't hear but it sounds like they're to himself so it doesn't really matter. He leads me into his bedroom and ushers me onto the bed. He picks up a Fleshlight and puts it onto my dick and carries on kissing me. I open my eyes and see that he's staring into mine deeply.

"You like it?"
"Yeah." I don't but whatever. I'm barely here anyway.
"You gonna fuck me now?"
"Yeah."

He turns over, slaps his hands onto his ass and pulls himself open. I still feel anxious but I'm really hard. He turns round to look at me to work out what the delay is and then watches as I put on a condom.

We fuck. First I fuck him from behind. Then I fuck him on his back. He rides me and I cum. We lie next to each other.

He tells me that he thinks he's addicted to sex, which he laughs about like it's a joke but then tells me about parties that he's been having and trying to organise. Sometimes they work and sometimes they don't. He posts his address online and says the times that he'll be free – usually in the middle of the night. He says that anyone can turn up and fuck him. Some nights nobody calls and others it gets busier. He says one night that twenty men were trying to fit into his small flat.

"I didn't even know who was fucking me anymore."

I apologise for not having any money and ask why he needed it. He said he owes someone for something. I think about asking him what his name is or maybe telling him mine, but decide not to bother. I ask him if he wants to fuck me, but he says he's not really into topping guys at the moment. He points to a dildo that's on the floor next to a pile of clothes and newspaper: "Sometimes I just top myself. Ha – sounds like I'm talking about suicide."

I could fall asleep, so I sit up to avoid it.

"Don't leave it so long next time, ok?" he says as I'm walking out of his place. "Don't be a stranger."

4

I catch a train to go and visit my friend for his birthday. I make arrangements to visit an artist who I've been asked to interview for an arts magazine that I've managed to get assignments from. I arrange so that I can interview her tomorrow, seeing how I'll still be in town.

I meet my friend in the coffee shop at the train station. He's lost weight. It's the first thing I notice about him. He hugs me.

"It's so good to see you."

He sits down at a table where he already has a drink. I walk to the counter and order. I return to the table. A splash of coffee spills onto my hand as I place the cup and saucer onto the table. I wipe my thumb and finger with a serviette and look at my friend, who is smiling.

"Thanks for coming," he says. "It should be fun."
"Where are we going?"
"There's a meal tonight – a Japanese place. Really nice and pretty cheap for what it is. After that we can go and party somewhere until someone dies."
"Sounds good."

After the coffee we move further into the city. We're sitting outside at a table so I can smoke. It's a really warm evening.

My friend is telling me about his recent breakup. It's been hard, mainly because his ex was an alcoholic. My friend is telling me

9

about how difficult it is to change someone; it's impossible, he says. He says how exhausted he is from worrying, even though he doesn't really have to anymore.

I'm wearing sunglasses and casually skimming through profiles on a cruising app. I see a guy who I slept with at the end of last summer who knew full well that he was HIV-positive and didn't say a word to me about it. The fear that engulfed me for the few weeks after the encounter – after the internet searching and cross-referencing had helped me find out about the guy's status, from a profile I found on a barebacking site, where the guy listed himself as a Pig, who was *"cum crazed and greedy for as many BB loads as his boy cunt could take"* – starts to return. I start to shake. I bite the inside of my mouth and take as deep a pull on my cigarette as I can. I look back at my friend through my sunglasses, not that my friend can tell. I ask my friend a question and then look back at my phone. My thumb hovers over the face of the guy from last summer who is smiling and in his one line description says he's "looking for fun". I try to think about what he'd say if I were to message and start talking to him. His profile says he's less than a mile away. I remember him saying that he worked somewhere round here, just after we'd fucked, but it feels too fucked up to end up this close to the guy in a city so big. I think about whether I should just send a message telling the guy to go fuck himself, or whether I should make the point that I had no idea that the guy was Positive and that he should have told me before we'd fucked because afterwards, even though my test came back negative, it was still fucked up and scary. There's a link to his Twitter account. I bookmark it and put my phone back in my pocket. I'm half tempted to stand up and apologise and say goodbye to my friend and get a train home and out of the city. Things feel too much.

"Stuff's just a bit of a mess," my friend says. "But I think it'll ultimately be good. Things generally turn out OK, don't they?"

We walk for about half an hour towards the restaurant where my friend's birthday party is going to be. When we get there a member of staff leads us to a round table in the corner of the room. As we make our way over, a woman waves and quickly walks over to my friend. They hug and she kisses him on the cheek. My friend introduces us to each other. I awkwardly kiss her on the cheek and sit down. A waiter comes over and we order drinks before my friend goes to the bathroom.

While my friend is in the bathroom I talk with the woman he's just introduced me to. We both say how we know my friend, where we met, how long we've known him. She met him through work. She says that she's been looking forward to meeting me because my friend has said lots of nice things about me. I tell her that the feeling is mutual even though I don't know if my friend has mentioned her before or not. I'm glad that my legs are underneath the table, so that no one can see them shaking.

My friend returns from the bathroom, stopping en route to greet three men who have just arrived at the restaurant. The four of them walk over to the table and sit down. My friend introduces them. Two of them are a couple. They sit down and start talking with my friend. They seem to know the woman as well – one of them, especially, who leans over and gives her a fond hug before he reaches over and shakes my hand.

The waiter brings drinks over and asks if people are ready to order food yet. My friend tells him that we're still waiting for a few more people.

I ask one of the guys from the couple how they know my friend.

"Umm, through friends pretty much," he says in a soft Spanish

11

accent. "We met like, a year ago or something – just around the scene, I guess," he laughs. "I think my friend was actually trying to set us up or something at first but when we met I think we got on too well to get into any of that stuff," he laughs again. "He's too skinny for me anyway," patting his boyfriend's leg.

The rest of my friend's guests arrive and we all order food. Before long, I'm drunk. I look across the table at my friend who is talking to a woman whose name I can't remember or didn't catch; they met through work, I can remember that much. She's wearing an oversized faded black t-shirt as a dress. There's a huge skull on the t-shirt. My friend orders more drinks. The girl takes a packet of cigarettes out from somewhere, a bag under the table. As she stands up, I pull a cigarette from my pocket and hold it up to her:

"Can I follow you?"

We walk outside.

"Are you having fun?"
"Yeah, it's nice." I feel more relaxed now that I'm outside. "I always find these kinds of things a little stressful."
"Lots of new faces and …" she says.
"Yeah and people who know each other and …"
"I don't really know anyone else either."
"Oh, okay. Cool. Same as me."
"Well, I've met that guy before – the one in the hat," she stoops for a second and nods her head in the direction of the restaurant window to point out a guy in an orange beany hat who is sat next to my friend and by the looks of it, telling a funny story.
"Oh ok. He seems nice."
"He's okay," she takes a drag on her cigarette and blows a mini mushroom cloud of smoke into the air. I'm suddenly struck by how huge the city looks behind her. Anonymity – being able to get lost;

it shoots through me, making me flinch.

"They're actually fucking each other. But I don't know if that's such a good idea." She pauses before she seems to realise that she needs to add a qualifier "For either of them really."
"Oh I didn't know that he was seeing anyone at the moment."
"I think it's pretty chilled out and stuff."
"Good, he needs a bit of fun and time to ... decompress or whatever," I pull a strange face as I realise how strange I probably sound but she seems aware or unaware of it because she says "Yeah I know you mean."
"How's he been recently? I've spoken to him on the phone and emails and stuff but I haven't seen him properly for ..." I trail off.
"He's getting there, I think." she says. I look at the torso-sized skull that she's wearing. It's eyes look deeper than they should or maybe it's just a really detailed design.
"Good. I love him a lot."
"Yeah, he's mentioned you a few times." I feel a buzz and have to suppress a giddy smile. "Oh cool." I look at my feet and smoke.
"You've been friends for years, right?"
"Yeah." The city continues to pulse.

There's a burst of movement and my friend's arm appears round my shoulder. The rest of the group move into our space.

"Happy fucking birthday to me!" my friend laughs and stumbles. "On and on we go!"

I try to ask who paid for my part of the bill but my words are lost. The girl I was talking to holds my arm and we start walking.

There seems to be a disagreement about where the group is supposed to be going. One of the guys throws his arms in the air, mock dramatically and then rubs my friend on his shoulders and

13

the group takes a left.

I want to take out my phone and look at the Twitter page that I bookmarked.

We walk into a bar just as a group of people is vacating a low down wooden table. I flop down onto a navy blue leather sofa, and force myself into its corner as the others sit down next to me and across from me at an identical sofa. The girl I was talking to and a couple of others go to the bar. Some more of my friend's friends who must have already been at the bar move over to the table and start hugging my friend and the others. I find myself shyly waving at a couple of people. My friend sits down next to me.
"Thank you so much for coming," he says to me, and then starts talking to someone else.

I open up the Twitter page of the guy from last summer. His profile picture is of him with his arms tied behind his back, on his knees smiling. The smile looks more like the sort of smile you'd see in a holiday photograph than in homemade pornography. His most recent post is a message to someone else:

:@_____ *Thanks for drilling my whole so good last night.*

The message he posted just before that says:
Waking up with someone else's cum oozing out of me. Best feeling eva!

I start scrolling through his posts and going back in time by using my thumb to push up the screen as the last couple of weeks of his life start to show in reverse order.

:*My boss just asked me why I'm tired LOL Can I say its cuz of the slamming party last night?!?* At the end of this Tweet there's an Emoji face laughing and crying.

14

:@_____ @_____ and @_____ who is gonna give this slut its first load tonight? At the end of this Tweet there's a purple devil Emoji, grinning.

:Can't be arsed with work today! Just wanna take loads! Need a new job!

:Bored, bored, bored. A sleeping Emoji with ZZZs coming out of its mouth.

:Any horny tops around the city centre? A couple of other users have favourite'd that Tweet but no one has replied.

While I'm looking at his account, I see that a new Tweet has appeared.

:Why does life have to be so complicated??? A sad Emoji face.

"Are you still here with us?" I look up at my friend, startled. I feel sick.
"Sorry,"

I end up giving a drunken blowob to one of my friend's work colleagues in the toilets of another bar. After he cums, I'm almost sick. I fall asleep on my friend's sofa to the sound of him fucking someone who he picked up in the last bar of the night. My phone runs out of battery as I scroll through the Twitter account of the guy from last summer, as I'm reading about the last Cumworship party that he attended:

:So many guys giving me their gift.

Blank.

5

I apologise for being late, as the assistant of the artist who I've arranged to interview let's me in to the studio. I almost cancelled but figured that for whatever reason, talking to her might help put things back into whatever place my instinct or subconscious is trying to tell me that they should be in.

The assistant leads me up some stairs to a large converted space that's about four times the size of my flat combined. One half of the minimal space is filled with sculptures and a long matte green table covered in papers and sketches and pencils and other art debris – the other half of the room is tidy and sparse.

The artist walks over and shakes my hand. I apologise for being late. The artist says that it's ok, although her polite reassurance doesn't put me totally at ease. She asks if it's ok if her daughter is present while we conduct the interview, which is fine. Her daughter, who the artist tells me for no apparent reason is fifteen, sits at the green table, consumed by her Macbook; she smiles at me and then looks back at the screen. We sit at the table a couple of spaces away from her, me on the same side of the table as her daughter and the artist opposite me on the other side. The artist asks her daughter if we're sitting too close.

"Are we going to distract you too much?"
"No," her daughter says with a shy smile. "It's fine."

"Did you have a late night?" the artist asks. I stay silent, until I realise that she's talking to me and not her daughter.
"Erm, yeah. Not really. A little late, yes."

The artist sends her assistant to fetch us some coffee. The assistant leaves the building rather than going to the kitchen. The wealth makes me feel uneasy.

We start talking about the artist's most recent show, which she tells me was a success. She seems friendly and I have to silently reassure myself that I'm projecting every other second when I feel like she hates me.

When her daughter leaves her computer to answer a call on her iPhone, which is covered by a Kawaii style cartoon ghost phone case, I'm able to briefly glimpse a Tumblr page, which she's been loading up with pictures. I can see that the title says *Dream Life of A Cutter.*

The interview seems to go well, as far as I can work out. The artist seems to warm to me more than I thought she was going to, or thought she had. She talks about how sculptures constantly change depending on your own specific space.

6

You've fucked me for days. I shit your cum. The bathroom smells of you – the scent follows me. You're inside me. I turn at angles that camouflage the stretch marks at the base of my stomach in the mirror and move onto the balls of my feet to amplify the weight that I can see that I've lost. Food has been functional, and is now running out. At the one point that I do leave your apartment and walk the short distance to buy cigarettes and fruit, the fresh air makes me nauseous, giddy. But my cock is still hard. I've lost count of the number of times that I've cum without you touching it – just from your dick sliding in and out of me at a pace that my body and senses can barely keep up with. It feels like you've been turning me inside out, a sharp, throbbing motion that is uncomfortable and transcendent at the same time. There have been hours when I've not had a single thought; I've only been able to feel. I've disappeared a thousand times and cum over and over and over again, while your spunk has coated my insides, become the only lubricant that I need, and my ass has been stretched to fit your cock so perfectly that it barely makes sense anymore.

My iPhone vibrates in my pocket. My jeans feel loose. Before long when you shake me and throw me around, I'll rattle. It's work. I don't answer because they'll hear the world around me, which would be misleading anyway, because at the moment my world is you and nothing much else. Some of your cum dribbles out my ass like a reminder. I put the phone back in my pocket and buy what I need to buy. I've got two more days before I need to see anyone.

I let myself back in. I walk up the stairs. The key to your apartment echoes in the lock. You've put a hoodie on and pulled the hood up but aside from that you're naked, sat at your laptop with your back to me. I put the cigarettes next to you on the desk, let you open them, pass one to me and then light one for yourself.

"There are a couple of other guys coming," you say. You turn the laptop so I can see a couple of photos, but they barely register. While my eyes zone out on the screen you stand up and lead me over to the sofa where you gently push me into sitting position. You crouch next to me and stroke my body with the back of the hand that you're holding your cigarette with.

The silence highlights something. Maybe how little we know about each other, in terms facts, like full names or jobs or whatever. I feel like you know me more than I know myself. I try to think of a question to ask but stop, realising how dumb it would be. I don't need to.

"Your hole is too perfect."

I move the astray onto the arm of the sofa and lean towards it. I'm semi-foetal so you can feel your way inside me. I look through the window at the city while I feel your finger move and slide in and out of me. A nicotine rush coincides with you putting more fingers inside me, which makes me shiver. It's this beautiful way of forgetting everything. By the time I'm looking at the ceiling, you're fucking me again. This time it's slower. I'm watching our shadows on the wall, and it feels like that's who is fucking, not us. I'm barely here anymore but I'm nowhere else either. You're easing your cock in and out and then deeper than it felt like you could, lifting my leg with one hand and pulling on my dick with your other. This time I cum fast but you just carry on and I stay hard anyway and you carry on doing the same.

7

There's a room of guys watching us fuck. Four … five? I'm so high that I've stopped caring or maybe didn't care in the first place. I can't remember, or just don't know. I'm the centre. I don't know whose hands are on me. Someone's tongue is inside my mouth, a cock has made its way into my hand, smudging pre-cum across my palm and fingers. The person kissing me sucks my tongue hard, like they want something from inside me. Their mouth is replaced with a cock. I feel out the shape with my lips and then lift my head so they can push inside me. You're still fucking me. You're speeding up which means you're going to cum soon. Your breath is racing. I start sucking the cock harder, get into a motion that matches the speed at which you're fucking me. Someone cums on my stomach.

8

I keep my eyes closed and listen to the city. I can pick out car engines separately, rather than as a hive, which tells me that it's morning. Footsteps on the wooden floor, a zipping sound, before you clear your throat and tell me that you have to go and that I have to leave. My eyes open on creases of your white bed sheets. I try to let them blur but you say it again.

I haven't got time to shower so I put on clothes that have existed almost entirely in a creased pile since I got here. I feel colder than when I was nude. I try to kiss you and you nod patronizingly and impatiently, so I try to make it down the steps and out of the building before you do. You wait because you want the same thing.

I feel like a ghost. Like if I were to take my feet of the floor I could just float or the wind would push me through the streets and cars could pass through while I was flinching for nothing. I'd still feel this nervous. The only good thing is that my phone battery is flat so no one can reach me, if anyone is trying.

I finally leave the city. My friend thinks I left days ago. I did a disappearing act with my life; only no one knew that the magic was happening.

9

When I walk back into my home I instantly walk to my bed. I kick a pile of post out of the way. The plants need watering. The air isn't fresh. I plug my iPhone in and hope that I can race to sleep before the charge wakes it up and it starts conveying things that people want me to know or do.

The first message is from a friend, asking me what I'm doing. I don't check the dates but I'm guessing that that the next few from her are spread out over the four days that I was gone. They're mostly the same, until the last one: *Call me when you get this. Are you ok? I'm worried.*

There are two voicemails. Small blue envelopes flash up. I check my emails by which I mean I look at them, don't open any new ones or read anything. I open Twitter and look at the page that I mentally obsessed over for the whole two-hour train journey home.

:Can someone and their friends do this to me and then use and abuse me? He's posted a picture of a young guy, maybe in his early twenties, wearing a hood that totally obscures his face. His face is being held down into the bed by a big muscle bear-type, while another similar guy is dripping cum into the young guy's ass, which is stuck up in the air. Two other guys are watching and masturbating.

:That moment when you listen to a song and the lyrics totally match yr life right now.

:Changed my profile photo! Has anyone noticed?? Sad face. *#justahintguys*

:I've only ever had on one proper date this century & that was when I was 18

& innocent! :(#amihideous

:I need coffee, breakfast and a sex boy master to fuck me full of his hot juicy spunk

:Wow. Just leaving a #cumpigparty – only in a bit of pain and had so much cock and cum. WIN!

:Headache tablet. Ketamine. Poppers. Prep – will that be enough for the #cumpigparty tonight PMSL #piglife

:5 hours till the #cumpigparty and I feel *slightly* better. Will cinderalla make the ball??

:I really hope the world ends tomorrow. I'm done with this shit. He posts an Emoji face of a yellow sad face, that looks like it's about to start crying.

:Just paid for my #cumpigparty ticket! So excited! #gangbangme #teambareback #piglife

:Hate not being able to buy my friends presents on their birthday. He posts a sad Emoji face.

10

I browse random websites to kill time while I wait for a guy to message back on a chat box I've got open on a cruising website. I see my own comment frozen: *Hey, how's it going?* The message is to someone who I've met before: this crazily handsome younger guy – twenty one according to his profile – who likes to suck guys off to completion and nothing else – he likes to swallow their cum or have it splashed over his face; he wants nothing in return. I tried to suck his dick once and there was nothing. He didn't get hard until I'd cum on his face. I feel disconnected when there's no way for me to please someone; it's this bizarre altruistic selfishness that doesn't make any sense. I'm an intensely fucked up person. I'm incapable of forging and maintaining healthy relationships because my attachments with people are so skewed to the point where if I don't feel like I have the entirety of someone's attention, heart and whatever my perceived idea of what *love* is, all of the time, then I automatically assume that that person is either lying to me, doesn't care about me or is somehow attempting to use me in ways that makes me hate them more than I could possibly try and sum up with these words without trailing off on some tangent longer than the one that I've already started to form in what would ultimately be a failed stab at creating a text that could somehow transmit to whoever is reading this right now just what a mess I am and this sentence isn't even a miniscule of the half of it. I could be as open with you as you want me to be and I'd still be hiding something. Every time I speak it feels like something is hidden within each new sentence that comes out of my mouth and for every sentence that comes out my mouth there's something that doesn't come out with even more meaning that's kept in.

Everyone has their own obsessions and I guess mine is trying to unlock as many as I can to try and find something that's still out of reach in terms of my understanding of it.

11

"Where the hell have you been? I thought you were dead or something. I was calling everyone. No one had seen you since the party. I almost called the police."

"Sorry,"

"You can't just disappear like that."

12

:*Had a quick/random Grindr hookup on the way to work. My colleagues don't know I've got raw spunk dribbling out my hole.*

:*Would love to be tied up and blindfolded in a fetish store.*

:*I hate come-downs. Any tips?*

:*FUCK. The. Weekend. Was. Insane.*

:*I've got the weekend off work for once! Any tops with a dungeon wanna work me over and even whore my holes out?* Smiling Emoji face.

:*I don't understand religion. Just saying.*

:*Just to be clear to some people: No, I'm not ashamed of liking & engaging in #barebacksex. I'm an adult, I know the implications.*

:*My friend was hurt and is in hospital – critical condition. 3:45am Friday night/Saturday morning in the gay village. If you saw anything please call Police.*

:*Too horny for today. Just cum for the 9th time. #thinkingbadthoughts*

:*Why have so many of my friends been asked to do porn but not me? Feeling left out.*

:*How is it that even when you are surrounded by people, you can feel completely alone?*

:I'd quite like to not exist anymore. Not a great feeling. An Emoji suicide made from a skull, an explosion, an Emoji with gritted teeth and an Emoji gun.

:The only downside of that? Knowing I won't have chance to take more today. Crying Emoji face.

:Waking up and remembering you've got an ass full of spunk. That.

:just got back from a #cumpigparty Strangers cum is dripping out of me. Best feeling in the world.

:I'm empty. I need to be full. #cumpig

:Met a boy last night. Swapped numbers. He's so cute. We're both bottoms tho. Sad Emoji face with tears.

:I just want fun.

:At home alone with a bottle of wine, wearing ankle cuffs and splayed waiting for a new friend to turn up.

:Does anyone know how to fuck properly?

:Who's up for some bb #cumpig fun tonight? I'm at the sauna, naked. ANYONE?!? Breed me.

:I'm in the sauna if anyone wants to come and say hello.

:Does anyone want to #pimpmyass out and film it *for real*?

:I finish my shift at 9. Any local masters have a dungeon they wanna invite me to?

:Don't get me wrong — pain is good sometimes LMFAO

:It takes skill to make me feel worthless without leaving me in total pain. Anyone?

:The best top I ever had treated me like this: He's posted a photo of a guy tied face-down with a pillow totally covering his head, while another guy is pushing his cock into him bareback. *#INEEDMORE*

13

I'm sat in the smoking section, outdoors at the back of the cruise bar. There are five wooden picnic benches; four of them are empty. I'm playing on my phone. I'm waiting for the bar to get busier. It's still early. People will be finishing work soon. I'm reading emails that are telling me that I'm late finishing articles and that there are still revisions that need to made on the pieces that I've already submitted. There's an opening of a new show tomorrow. I decide that I'll go. It's this queer painter that I like. I like his work. I don't know much about him as a person although I once saw him at a cruise bar where no one recognized him. I didn't speak to him.

I read a text from a friend who asks me how I am. I decide that I'll reply later. I can't think of anything to write.

The bench shakes. A drunken guy in his sixties sits down.

"How's it going?" he does this strange movement with his mouth, like he's cleaning his teeth with his tongue, his damp lips contort weirdly for a second.
"I'm good," I say. "Are you having fun?"
"No." the man deadpans, and then laughs loudly and suddenly hits the table with his hand. I flinch. He mumbles a half word and then repeats himself and asks me if *I'm* having fun. It takes him a couple of attempts to get his eyes level with mine. I can smell the alcohol on his breath.

"Yeah, I'm good, thanks," I try and speak as clearly as I can. I don't know if he can hear me properly.
"You're ok are ya? Good, good," he drinks and rolls his eyes back

so I can see nothing but white for a second, like a kid trying to pull what they think is an ugly face.

"You don't mind me sitting here, do you? You don't mind me sitting with you?"

"No – it's fine," I try to smile in a way that will make me look more relaxed than I actually am. I want to leave but the idea of hurting the man's feelings is painful.

"So," I realise I'm repeating myself but I finish the sentence anyway because nothing really matters. "Have you had a good time?"

The old man scrunches up his face and gives an exaggerated shrug, like he's on stage in a pantomime. "It's ok," he leans into the table. "How about you?"

"Yes thanks," I don't want the conversation to veer towards sex. "I haven't been here long – I just came in to have a drink and a smoke." I light another cigarette. "I like it here – it's pretty chilled out."

"Have you not had any fun in there?" The old man cocks his head in the direction of the door back into he club.

"No. I don't think I'm really in the mood."

"I don't blame you!" the man laughs suddenly again, bangs the table. I flinch again.

There's a pause. I pretend to look at my phone.

"I've had a little play," says the older guy, lowering the tone of his voice slightly. When he speaks quieter he slurs his words less. "In the darkrooms – you know."

"Cool." I look back at my phone but try to make it look natural so it doesn't just appear as if I'm trying to get rid of the man, which I'm hoping he will do himself.

"Have you had a play yet?"

31

"No," I realise that a shade of impatience made its way out but I guess that the man is probably too drunk to pick up on it.

There's another pause – the longest since the conversation started.

"I'd like to have a play with you." The man leans in closer and stops, it looks like he's been frozen and left hovering.

"Oh, right," I look up from my phone. "No. I'm ok, thanks. I'm sure someone in there will sort you out though."

The man sits back quickly and puts his hands up, head tilted to the side like he's refusing to let someone else pay for dinner. "No, no, it's fine, no worries, it's fine." His tone lowers again and he tries to move on to the next subject but he doesn't know what it is or what it might need to be. He looks like he might cry. "No, no, it's fine. I've had a little play already."

I put my phone in my pocket. I pick up my box of cigarettes. Before I can stand up to go inside, the man starts talking again.

"So are you gay or bi?" The man nods as if I've has already started answering. The words don't seem to fit him. He doesn't look comfortable asking or talking about that kind of thing.

"Gay, I suppose." I'm surprised at how certain I sound. That sort of thing can never be properly defined but I know that's not a conversation that can be had at this point in time.
"Oh yeah." The man is still nodding.
"You?" I feel obliged to ask.
"I'm bi these days." Again, the words don't fit the man. The word "bi", in particular, doesn't seem to suit his voice. "That's only a recent thing though – last couple of years, you know." The man hold up his hand and waggles a finger with a wedding ring on it.

"Oh okay …"

"I'd honestly never even thought about doing anything with a man – my whole life."

"Right," I feel sad.

"I was never homophobic or anything like that," again a word that sounds plausibly new for the man. "I was married and I … I mean, I *love* women. You know, what I mean?" he laughs and his hand trembles as he picks up his drink and glugs. "I got married when I was twenty and I never even once wanted to do anything with any men. I loved fucking women."

"Right."

"But my wife died," the man laughs louder than he has so far. There are tears in his eyes. Two men sit at the table next to us. The man's laugh turns into what sounds like a moan. The man rolls his head round his shoulders as if he's stretching and looks on the brink of crying. "She died."

"I'm sorry to hear that."

"Oh it's alright …"

"It must have been really hard."

"The thing is … haha … you still get horny, you know?"

I try to reply but feel lost and so the result is a noise that's somewhere between the word *yeah*, a half laugh, and a sniff of the nose.

"So I slept with prostitutes, but I can't afford that. And I met a couple of blokes off the internet – just got my dick sucked, you know. Then I fucked a couple of 'em. Then I started coming here and getting fucked myself, haha."

I don't know what to say. The old man is crying. The two guys who had sat down next to us get up and go back inside the bar.

The old man leans in and holds his drink towards his torso, towards his heart and hangs his head close to me.

33

"It's not fucking fair." He's sobbing while he talks, a string of spit linking his lips and snot starting to foam from his nose. "It's not fair. I just missed her. I missed having sex. I missed being with someone. I missed touching someone. It isn't fair. I only did it because I needed … I only did it a few times and now I've fucking got it, haven't I? I only did it a few times. I got HIV the second time I got fucked. I mean, fucking hell, *it isn't fair.*"

I start to shake. I put my hands under to the table to hide the shaking. The man looks like he's talking to someone who isn't there. Maybe I'm not. He's so lost. His eyes are glazed.

"I work my whole life – I tried to be good, I tried to be a good husband – I tried to look after my kids and raise 'em properly when they were young and I fucking end up *like this.*" The man shows his teeth. He looks angry now. He's practically snarling.

The man puts his head in his hands. The conversation is over and I don't know what to say. The man doesn't move. He looks like he could stay there forever.

14

:Just fucking rape me already. LOL

15

I meet someone for a drink. He's hired a hotel so that we can fuck. We started talking on a fetish website. He's listed as an 'Aggressive Top'. I'm listed at 'Versatile', which is pretty much how my whole existence could be summed up; or maybe a passive-aggressive-versatile although it wouldn't make sense when it came down to sex. I'm malleable and I just want to be within the desires of whoever I want to want me. He's getting drunk and slightly snappy. He tells me that he's going to hurt me. *Good*, I say. He tells me that I won't be able to walk for days, but he says this as a joke. I tell him to do his worst. He says he's going to make me scream and beg for mercy. I say please. He says that all I am is a body that's there for him to act out his own personal fantasies on. I say that's fine. He says he wants me unconscious. I say that I'm happy to play dead. He asks if he can put Rohypnol in my drink. I say yes. He does. We agree to leave straight away so that I don't pass out until we get to the room that he's booked.

16

I walk into the show that I'm supposed to review, with a black eye from where you punched me last night. It's sore enough for people to stare although how many are staring and how many are looking right through me is hard to say because I'm feeling so paranoid that I'm half expecting you to jump out from behind a door an tell me that I'm still just dreaming and when I wake up you're going to want to fuck me again.

The main focal point of the exhibition is a piece entitled Mooning and Craft, which is made up of a split screen film projected onto a large blank wall in the gallery. The left hand side of the film shows a grainy black and white video of a spaceship just after its launch; a billowing tail of fuel trailing behind as the vessel flies diagonally out of view before the images loop again from the start. The right hand side of the screen uses the same footage, only it stops and starts, rewinds randomly, so that halfway into its ascent, the rocket is dragged back by video manipulation, then it shoots quicker only to halt and rewind again. The rocket is in a constant state of failure and repetition – I make a note of that on my phone, I also make the obvious reference to sex, how it could be alluding to penetration, but the main thing that it seems to be screaming out at me is a theme of regret; the wish that we could change something the instant that we do it, the second when it becomes apparent that we're not able to put a halt to things – we get carried away so often – things are accelerated and there's no way to stop.

I approach the artist with my notes, half memorized and half vague, due to the drugs or the drink, or the fact that I got a text just as I was about to put my iPhone into my pocket that just read

Hi. Remember me from … and details of some bar where I've met and fucked whoever texted, but I don't remember and I don't know.

"That's an interesting interpretation," the artist says. "I guess I was more interested in the idea of space and how an object impinges on that. To me, it touches on ideas of ownership, property, intangible emotions being physicalized, more than any personal …" She trails off as someone from Artforum walks over and distracts her. She's gone. I'm half annoyed with her but angrier with myself for glazing over when she gave her response. The fact that she implied I was wrong shook me and hurt me so much that I switched off any remaining critical faculties, meaning I have barely any understanding or even recollection of what she said, five seconds after she said it, meaning that my review will be way off point, and this is just a tiny example of how weak I am right now.

I smile at one of the gallery assistants who I think I've seen on one of the cruising apps at some point but he just winces when he sees my black eye before manners remind him how he needs to act and he gives a faintest of smiles back.

I leave the gallery and try to let the annoyance and embarrassment caused by the aloofness of the artist and my frustration at my own ability to concentrate settle. I stop at the bottom of the short stack of stone steps that lead up to gallery, light a cigarette and check a cruising app.

Someone near says *hey.*
Hi
Wuu2
Nothing you?
Nothing. Horny.
Where ru?
City centre.

38

I'm by the Tentacle Gallery.
2 streets away.
What are you in to?
Fucking. Versatile. Like it rough. Like to be rough.
Can you accommodate?
Yes. He sends me his address, which I open on Google Maps. He sends me a code to get into the building that his flat is in. *My door is on the latch. Hurry.*

A guy asks me for change and I jump. His face looks like it's been caved in. I put my phone in my pocket quickly and give him the couple of coins that my knuckles brush against.

I open Google Maps again. I'm the blue circle that's moving and he's a red stationary dot. The streets align more as I get closer to him. I look up every so often to avoid bumping into people but mostly I'm just staring at my iPhone, which has become part of my sweaty hand.

Hurry.

I key in the security code in the silver pad at the bottom of the red brick building. I enter and get the elevator up until I'm on the right floor.

I walk into the small but immaculate studio flat and see him on all fours naked except for a jock strap. I can see that his ass is already lubed because of the way the moisture is shining. He half looks at me, closes his eyes and faces forward away from me.

"Hurry."

I put the chain lock on the door and start to take off my clothes as quickly as I can, holding my breath – for some reason I don't want to breathe too loudly. I walk over to the bed and put my hands either side of his ass. There are no condoms and he doesn't mention them so I just start fucking him.

I feel like I could cum straight away. He makes this gentle inward moan, like a purr. I slide back out and then back in a few times, which is easy.

"You're my fourth load tonight," he whispers. "I need your cum."
I start to fuck harder, almost out of fear.
"I want to be fucked by strangers forever."

Things start to feel more desperate so I fuck him as hard as I can. The bed shakes and he puts his head down onto the pillow, like he's crying into it. He moves his head to the side so that one eye is covered by the pillow and his other is turning as far as it can, wide open, trying to see me, trying to look at me properly for the first time but he gives up fast and his whole face is covered.

"I fucking love you. I'm in love with your dick."

17

— A photograph of an American Apparel sign.
— A gif of Lindsay Lohan smoking a cigarette and blowing the smoke to the side.
— A photograph of a pale girl with Sea-Punk style coloured hair.
— A cat on a fluorescent pink and green background with 'FUCK YOU' written in Comic Sans.
— A screen-grab of an iPhone message that says 'If we ever have sex I'm gonna moan your URL'.
— What looks like an art installation where there are three square black televisions balanced on top of each other, each of them playing static.
— A gif of two teenagers kissing a girl biting a boys lip.
— A black and white photograph of a male model called Ash Stymest, shirtless and looking melancholic.
— A box of Marlboro Red cigarettes, which has been doctored so that the health warning on the front reads 'You're going to die anyway'.
— A gif of a waterfall.
— A gif of a YIN YANG sign leaking black droplets.
— Cara Delevingne wearing a WU TANG CLAN T-shirt.
— Jonathan Brandis aged 8.
— A screenshot from the computer game, DOOM.
— A gif of Alice Glass from Crystal Castles screaming.
— A gif of people dancing in the Daft Punk anime video.
— A severed head from a horror film.
— Two people having sex in the middle of a riot.
— A suburban American house.
— Freddy Krueger flashing the blades on his fingers.
— A high-rise council flat in the UK.

— Two skinheads kissing.
— A tattoo of a cannabis leaf on someone's neck
— The Bone Church in Kutná Hora.
— A VHS of Heathers.
— DO YOU LOVE ME written in neon letters
— A Microsoft Windows 95 logo.
— A Nintendo Gameboy covered in paint.
— Michael Jackson posing with Macaulay Culkin and Bubbles the chimp.
— The Kardashians taking the Ice Water Bucket Challenge.
— A gif of some day-glow font floating back and forth that says 'WALKS INTO THE CLUB LIKE … *CHECKS PHONE*'.
— A spiked dog collar and some handcuffs.
— The words 'STAY RAD' flashing in different colours over and over again.
— A Terence Koh sculpture made of cocaine.
— A black and white gif of two men fucking. They're both muscular and you can't see their faces.
— River Phoenix in Stand By Me.
— The word FUCK superimposed onto a photograph of some flowers.
— An ecstasy tablet with a Smiley face etched into it.
— Wiz Khalifa smoking a joint.
— A reply to an anonymous question that says: *'i don't know if that's true but thank you for saying that. i don't cut so much anymore but there are some days when it seems like it's the only thing that makes sense. i see everyone else and they're beautiful and it only makes me feel worse. i don't know. thanks for writing that though even though at this point in my life it doesn't feel like i'm ever going to be able to believe it. hope i don't sound like too much of a dick'*
— A photograph of a Nike t-shirt that's been altered so that above the swish it sakes TRILL.
— **Anon:** *Why aren't there any photos of you on here?*
— **Dreamlifeofacutter:** *How do you know there aren't?*

Anon: Because I've seen you in real life.

Dreamlifeofacutter: IRL LOL

Anon: You should work in the arts when you're older. You've got such a good curatorial eye for arrangement and the way you present images is just stunning. You're very talented. I'm worried that you might not realise it — but you're amazing, ok? And never let this world tell you that you're not.

Dreamlifeofacutter: PMSL

18

I spend the evening waiting for someone who isn't going to come. I open my laptop and read the latest posts on a barebacking message board.

Users post details of the unprotected sex that they've had. They're bragging.

There's a thread for people to post their tallies, meaning how many times someone has cum inside them, so far this year. One user says: *so far it's only 29. Not as good as this time last year but I've still got time to make it up. I wish I could quit my job because it's holding me back from being my true self, what I was created to be which is one hundred per cent, twenty-four hour a day cum dump. My only calling is to be a total bottom pig, with my mancunt designed to take as many raw loads from as many top guys as I can. I don't care who it is. I'm addicted. Maybe I should start writing my resignation now.*

Someone replies: *Spoken like a true, proud bottom. We know what our job is. We know what we have to do. My tally so far is 64, most of them from Poz'd up guys like myself. Nothing better than falling asleep knowing that my hole is overflowing with toxic juices.*

The next post: *I'm a poz'd up piggy, too. If only my boss knew why I had to call in sick the other day – I said it was a stomach upset when really it was because of the comedown from a Slamming party where my worthless hole was the main attraction. Can't wait to see the video! Even when I'd passed out, Poz'd up guys carried on breeding my hole. Such a proud moment. Looking forward to seeing it because I sure as hell can't remember it.*

19

I wake up at 1:30am and instantly look for you. You're sitting at the desk where your computer is, snorting a line of bluish-white powder. Your face is lit by the pornography that you're watching.

"So are we going out?"
"I guess ..."

Twenty minutes later and I'm washing my hands and face in your bathroom with the light off.

Thirty minutes after that, we're sat in a cruising bar. The only real light is from a set of small red bulbs in the middle of the room, where the drinks are served. Occasionally we see a face that we recognize or someone will recognize us but we keep it low key and just nod.

You stand up and finish your drink. You start walking towards the darkrooms, where the majority of the sex happens. I walk behind you and brush my hand against the back of your jeans as we walk in. It accidentally feels like a reminder.

I let me eyes adjust to the darkness.

Eventually I can flesh out shadows with features but it's still vague. Someone starts to kiss me. A hand slips up my t-shirt. I reach to the side to check that you're still there, which you are. The same person has a hand planted round your crotch – my fingers trace the arm down to your jeans, which are still fastened. You move suddenly, which makes me move too – my hands feeling out the wall behind me. It dawns on me how high I am and how much I've been relying on the light for balance. My brain and my eyes feel like trapeze artists.

We push though a set of hanging plastic strips that separate the first darkroom from a small area split into six cubicles, some with glory holes and some without. It's still dark but there's a dim glow and it's not as black as the room that we've just stepped out of.

The way that the space is split with a slim corridor running between the cubicles reminds me of a level from a computer game and the fake industrial pipes on the wall add to it. A guy stands at the end of the walkway, with two cubicle doors either side of him, his hand resting on his belt buckle. You walk towards him and I follow. The man leans forward and kisses you. You put your hand back and hold mine, which surprises me. I touch your back. I realize how thin you've got. I run my fingers over your shoulder blades. The guy kisses you harder, and pulls you forward, holding the sides of your head. He starts sidestepping into one of the cubicles, guiding you as you kiss. You let go of my hand and follow the guy in. You close the door.

I hear a belt being undone and your breath speeding up as you kiss him.

A hand touches my ass. It reaches round and starts feeling the front of my legs and then my dick, which isn't hard. Someone starts kissing the back of my neck. I close my eyes and turn round.

I let the stranger steer me towards a cubicle. I hold out a hand for balance. When it brushes against plastic I realizes I've been led back into one of the darkrooms; I open my eyes but it's pointless: there's nothing.

I trip but stay on my feet. The floor feels sticky. The guy who brought me in is rough. I feel stubble scrape against my cheek as the guy starts kissing my neck again. I can feel the guy's heart. It's going fast. Hands run up and down my back like he can't decide what to do with me, or what to do first. My head bumps against a wall. My belt is unfastened clumsily. A hand covers both my wrists and holds them up against the wall. A tongue fills my mouth, pushes the back of my front teeth uncomfortably. Another hand goes up my t-shirt. Someone else is pulling my jeans down round my ankles. Something's pushed in my face, bending my nose, a hand with a bottle or a tube or … I snort whatever it is and a fast daze lands quickly, blurring the nothingness further. My head nods onto my right shoulder but is quickly pulled back up again and kissed hard. I'm bent over. A finger muddles round my ass. That finger quickly becomes a cock. I make a sound somewhere between a cry, a choke and a cough as whoever's dick enters me. There's no condom. Someone else is pulling at my hair. My scalp feels tight. The guy fucking me does it hard. It hurts. Two cocks try and get into my mouth, vying for space. I can feel another couple rubbing against my stomach. I feel the stitching of my t-shirt rip under one arm. It sounds like I can hear crying – the guy fucking me? But the music seems so much louder now. Repetitive beats and someone singing something about needing someone forever till the end of time. It's hard to make out anything else. The cock isn't in me anymore. I'm on the floor. I remember falling as it actually happens. Time's a mess. I'm too high. Someone's shouting. The beats of the song begin to stretch. I think it was me who was crying. Things are a lot heavier. I'm pulling my jeans back up to my waist. It takes effort - more than you'd think. Stuff is dense – stuff like air. I'm nodding out and I'm being fucked again. I open my eyes and I'm back on the floor. There's a synthetic taste in the back of my throat, like gone off medicine. I feel a vibration in his pocket. I reach in to get my phone. I realize how wet my hands are and wipe them on my leg and take the phone out. I press a button and the small rectangle that's from a friend I haven't spoken to for a few days and that says: *hope yr ok. xxx* is such a contrast to the darkness that it lights up the room for two seconds. Through a squint I see a heavyset guy in his fifties buttoning up a shirt, a guy in his twenties leaning against a wall with his eyes closed and playing with his dick and trying to make himself hard, there's two older guys standing close to each other with their trousers down, some others too, but the light soon leaves.

I make my way back into the bar. The sudden amount of clear space throws me. I order a drink and can't tell if the guy behind the bar is looking at me weirdly. I try to make better eye contact, but that makes it worse. I'm still squinting. When I scratch my nose my hand comes back with blood on it. I think I can hear you being fucked but it might just be the music. Things feel knotted.

20

— Leonardo DiCaprio circa Romeo and Juliet, wearing a Hawaiian style shirt, loading a revolver.
— A gif of the words DON'T BE FUCKING RUDE, written in purple bubble writing, floating on the page like they're balanced on a wind.
— An anime character with big sad eyes, with pink petals falling around her face.
— A grainy photo of Kathleen Hanna, taken from an old fanzine, superimposed onto an animated background of floating kisses and love hearts.
— A picture of a watermelon.
— Re-Blog if you're accepting anonymous asks from anyone about anything.
— A bottle of prescription medication that has been Photoshopped so that the label says Ketamine.
— **Anonymous:** *I wish you lived closer because we could totally hang out.*
— **Dreamlifeofacutter:** *We need an escape plan!* I wish I could just vanish!
— A photo of a stationary black butterfly.
— A film still: two people in the shower, what looks like a mans hand wrapped round a woman's back with subtitles that say "If you don't love me, you can still fuck me."
— Cara Delevigne on a catwalk.
— Someone holding a Chanel bag.
— A close up photo of two pieces of sushi.
— A bitmap ice-cream cone.
— A photograph of a boy with a tattooed neck and a sweatshirt with a Nintendo logo on it laughing in front of a hazy city

sunset.
— The words EPIC FAIL written in bitmap.
— A picture of the band Crystal Castles.
— A gif of the old MTV logo from the 1990s, with changing colours.
— Some tarot cards.
— A picture of a Vans skate shoe.
— Lindsay Lohan leaving a restaurant with friends.
— A stylised photo of cup of Starbucks coffee next to a Krispy Kreme donut tray.
— A sunset.
— Capital letters that read: MESSAGES PLEASE?
— A girl with lots of red lipstick, in an oversized grey sweatshirt with a picture of Mickey Mouse on it, leaning towards the camera and pulling an expression that looks like it's meant to be half cute/half sexy and is/isn't depending on whoever looks at it.
— A photograph of a Japanese woman with orangey/blonde hair. Someone has edited a rectangle of crass purple/orange/blue/green Spectrum style graphics that keep changing, and put it across the picture so that it blocks out her eyes.
— A close-up photograph of some pink Prozac tablets.
— A $100 note with a black and white photo of Nicki Minaj pasted over where the president's head usually is.
— A picture of Tyler, The Creator holding a skateboard.
— A photorealist painting of a wolf and a waterfall.
— Tiny writing in italic red lettering that says: you give me goose bumps.
— A photo of a teenage boy with a floppy fringe pretending to be scared of and cower away from a life-size model of one of the ghosts from Pacman.
— Two teenage punks with heavily tattooed torsos, fucking, in black and white.
— Three inverted crosses.

— The words: DESTROY WHAT DESTROYS YOU superimposed onto some clouds.
— An animated gif of Bill Cosby. Someone has edited it together so it looks like he's mouthing the words: DIE, CUNT.
— A shot from Beetlejuice, when Geena Davis's character has transformed herself into a monster by stretching out her mouth and putting her eyes on her tongue.
— A photo of a cherry blossom tree.
— A renaissance painting.
— A stylish looking Japanese girl wearing huge headphones.
— An elaborately drawn Guro drawing of a girl whose face has been cut open down the middle so that her skull is exposed and blood is exploding out. Flies buzz about in the wound.
— A fried egg with the yolk Photoshopped green.
— Alice Glass from Crystal Castles wearing a Smiths t-shirt.
— The boy with the rabbit ears from Harmony Korine's film Gummo, sitting on a bridge smoking.
— A photograph of Lindsay Lohan that looks like it was taken to promote the white jacket that she's wearing. She's standing side on and she's holding the collar of the jacket and her mouth is open. She's pouting a little and you can see her teeth.
— A gif of a nude bitmap woman sitting on the side of a bitmap bed smoking a cigarette and looking away from a nude bitmap man who is lying and trembling.
— A painting by the queer artist whose show I forgot to go to.
— 2014 SUXXX sprayed on a brick wall.
— A photo from a cruising bar under which someone has left a comment comparing it to a level from one of the DOOM video games. Someone else says LOL.
— Weeds growing round a punctured car tyre.
— A gif of a house burning down.

21

I write a review of a show that I never went to. I write an interpretation of paintings that I haven't seen. I talk about colours that I'm unsure of. There's nothing about it on the internet yet, so it's hard to know what to say. I look at the private view invitation and the minimal information on the gallery website and use that to form an impression of an opinion. Firm opinions never seem legitimate, anyway. Nobody knows anything for sure. I'm never convinced that people mean anything that they say to anyone else. Most of the things that I think to myself – as in *really think* to myself, when I'm not trying to reject what my brain is giving to me – I'd never want to say out loud; for the sake of others, for myself.

There are two photographs of two paintings on the gallery website, which I think is enough to go on in order to make an overall judgment of the artist and his whole line of thinking at this moment in time.

I write down my thoughts – which is different to thinking, I guess. I write that the paintings seem to present themselves as knowing that they are paintings. I say that that the colours and images remove themselves from anything else other than what is in each respective painting and in doing so detach themselves enough to – perversely – be able to take in influences from everything other than paintings. I say that I can see the internet, I can see bodies; the smudges of shapes vague enough to be abstract but clear enough to show the movements of sex, and of pop references. Everything is at once recognizable and new, but still manages to rest on the past in a self-conscious but confident way.

I write that the recognition of the acceleration of modern culture allows all sorts of slight of hand magic tricks – the artist is able to be joyous, sarcastic and sincere at the same time. I stop typing because I feel I so lost.

I walk to the window and open it up. I rest my arms on the window ledge and look at the buildings around where I live. I wish they were bigger, like in bigger cities, and wander how hurt I would be if I were to throw myself out. I look at the ground and feel sick. I think about the force of the stationary pavement, holding firm and almost pushing up as gravity throws my body into it. I think of the walls closing in on a character in an adventure film, gravity being one and the ground being another – would one be moving faster? You'd think it would be gravity but I think the ground, and the sky too for that matter, are constantly doing magic tricks that we never spot or if we do we only catch glimpses of, so in short: who knows?

I stop looking. I hate heights. It occurs to me that when people are scared of something it's only because they don't trust themselves.

You can always pick out shadows and the feeling that people are there when they're not. I say this about the paintings. I focus on one of the photographs of the paintings which could be interpreted as a crowd scene – there are no definite people on there but it looks like there could be several heads – people eating a meal, but the smears of the acrylic make it look more sensual or specifically sexual: a group sex scene. I talk about the artist using paintings as a queer space in which meaning and facts and specifics are bent out of shape and displaced by a dream-logic where things make emotional sense as opposed to narrative sense. The painting feels real. It doesn't feel binary, I write that. I think that I think it too, but I'm losing track of what I really think. It always happens when I try to explain my thoughts to other people or in this case to whoever is reading this.

22

There are days when I don't think I need you and I'm happy. I am at my happiest when I am on my own. It's hard to explain that to people because they take it as insult. When I tell someone that my favourite person to spend time with is myself, then I know it sounds miserable or crazy but only through the filters that we've been forced to grow up viewing things through.

Some of my greatest sexual encounters have been in dreams or in fantasies. I think my best sexual moment is the memory that I've got of a real sexual situation that I was in. It was great in real life but it's *really* beautiful in the memory.

When I think, I can reconstruct things in intricate ways and pick out the moments that I missed when they were actually happening. When I focus on them I realize how much weight and power that minute details actually carried. Certain facial expressions, a look in your eyes – the pattern of your breathing: things get so lost when you're doing them for real. How can I reconstruct those memories in real life again? I want to fit into a real life memory as it's happening and stay there, like I'm trapped and ecstatic in a gif of the greatest moment that I've ever felt that I'll be able to feel forever. I want to be swallowed by the sea.

23

:Having bad thoughts.

:I just turned 30. Am I too old to do porn?

:There are no where near enough hours in the day for me to meet all of my sexual needs. I hate the twenty-four hour clock! LOL

:I WISH THIS WAS ME. He posts a photo of a guy with his legs stuck in the air. He is surrounded by four other guys who are all dripping their cum onto and into his asshole.

:Should I buy an open mouth gag?

:Exhausted from last night at the Cum Worship event. Thanks to all the tops who fed their piggy.

:Any top who pulls out before he cums is not a real top. #whataletdown #cumpig

:I'm off work for a week. Who wants to fill me?

:Retweet if you want to dump some seed inside me.

:That feeling when it turns out a friend is actually just an acquaintance.

:Thinking of getting a tattoo. Maybe ENTER written above my hole?!? LOL. An Emoji face that's crying with laughter.

:I woke up so horny today. #needbarebacksexnow

:So do I stay home tonight or head to a sex club? Thoughts please people ...

:In dire need of cash and raw loads of cum.

:WILL ANYONE BE WILLING TO PIMP ME OUT AND USE ME AS THEIR PERSONAL WHORE AND FILM IT?

:So my friend died last night. Feel so sad. A line of three Emoji faces, all crying.

:Any sadistic tops out there who are also financially well off and feeling generous? I'm kind of desperate. #pimpmeout

:My shoes are covered in piss and my ass smells of spunk. #musthavebeenagoodnight

:The best mornings are when I wake up in a hotel with cum dripping out of me.

:My total stress levels right now would need to be measured on the Richter Scale. #howcanichangethings

:I have the whole day off. Anyone fancy a visit to the sauna with me?

:I want to try my first double penetration with two poz guys. Anyone up for it?

24

There are the days when you disappear. I can see you've read my messages but then you're gone. I'll look at my phone and see your name with the number of phone calls I've tried making to you - nineteen, twenty - none of which you've picked up. I'll ask you if you're having a good day or if everything is cool. If I'm lucky, hours later I'll get a one-word response: "Yes," or at a push, "Yes thanks." There's never any explanation as to where you've been. There doesn't need to be. I know you've been with him. I know you've been with them. I know that your phone has been silenced, ignored, drowned out by the sound of fucking in hotels, the sound of the music in the loud bars in which you're being seduced or in which you are seducing. I know that you cancel the calls and that they probably ask you about who it is that's trying to get in touch with you so manically. I can see that it's crazy. I can tell that I'm insane. I get it. I know that we are all supposed to be alone. I know that I am supposed to be alone. But when I think of you in their arms, when I'm sat wanting you – that's when I start to lose it. That's when I can't bear to just sit there. When I'm in their arms it's fine, it's ok. So it's basically just all about this finely-tuned jealousy and paranoia that we can fool ourselves into thinking is balanced out by the company and the approval of others. Fuck it. We're fucked.

25

I'm too drunk to stand in the darkroom. I work my way outside to the smoking section. I sit down. I light a cigarette. I start to cry.

Someone puts his arm round me. They don't speak. A hand gently squeezes my shoulder. I'm shaking. I'm crying so hard. Life seems inescapable, mainly because I can't say what I need to escape from; I don't know. There are practical things that could be better and there are emotional states that I'd prefer to be a lot different but when I try and parse through each element objectively it's hard to figure out what's going wrong. On their own, not one thing is bad enough to make me want to vanish or die or just … stop. And when I whizz through them all like a pile of cards, I can't identify any specific combination. Then there's this anger that I feel when I think about the advice that other people would give me – they'd say it was easy to see what things I needed to stop doing – and even just thinking that makes me want to scream and start scratching at myself so hard until flesh starts to rip. Nothing is simple, everything is complicated, and life is about managing to accept that without getting crushed by it first. Within all of that mess, there's such beauty. I know that. I feel it. It's just in the lags and dips that things become frightening.

"He's not worth it, whoever he is," says the person who is hugging me. The fact that whoever this is immediately thinks that this is something to do with love or loneliness, makes me cry harder. I hear a sound come out of my mouth. I feel angry but it just turns into more sadness.

I want the reassurance of his company at the same time that I want him to feel bad about making assumptions. I'm fucked up and it's just the sort of thing that I half accept about myself and half hate myself for.

I tell him that my boyfriend killed himself because it makes me feel unimpeachable. I tell him that he was horrifically depressed – the sort of depressed that people really just can't understand. The really complicated depressed. I also tell him that he was dyslexic. I tell him that in my boyfriend's last few months, he'd constantly be asking me how to spell certain words, or he'd ask me about various pieces of punctuation – how certain sentences were supposed to work – without ever revealing what sentences he was working on. I tell him that I was inadvertently helping my boyfriend to write his suicide note.

I tell him that on the day I found my boyfriend hanging from a homemade noose, with a knot that reminded me of a plaited bread roll that you might see in an upmarket bakery, the Biro scrawled note taped to the front of his t-shirt felt more like a conversation with myself than a farewell from him.

When I get that far I to stop talking so freely. I don't go into discussing the actual content of my boyfriend's suicide note. I drop hints about it, and make vague comments about it, but don't go any deeper than that. There are always so many different versions of how things happened, whether they happened or not. I say enough to make sure that he's left with the impression that whatever was contained in the suicide letter must have been really heavy – and not just because of the obvious. It's hard to explain – especially when I feel so lost and wasted and fucked – but I want him to know that the suicide note wasn't just a usual example of its genre: sad, tragic, whatever; I want him, I *need* him to know that as well as all that stuff, it was *profound*.

"Fuck."

It's working, I think. I feel better, maybe because of the attention I'm getting, I guess. It's best I don't try and work it out or do anything else that might devalue this feeling that I need so much right now.

It feels important to only give him so much. I want him to feel like there are questions that he needs to ask me but that he won't because he can tell I won't be able or want to answer. That way – I won't just feel like an outline that he can see straight through, that hasn't been coloured in. Things need to be greyer, more of the time. I think it's probably like the emotional equivalent of being media savvy. I want him to know or to think – I'm not sure what the difference is, not that it matters – that I'm just one of those really emotionally dense and complicated people that no one will ever really fully understand because, well I don't know, probably because the very basics of the matter are: I'm not.

I don't want to be blamed for anything.

I have all of these ideals. I tell him that my boyfriend and I met at a concert. There was a guy onstage in tears screaming this really amazing song about some dark sexually abusive relationship. I tell him that my boyfriend and I just started kissing. There was no verbal language between us. We were standing next to each other, and had noticed each other a couple of times. There was some sensual psychic telepathy shit in the air, I tell him, and we just clicked without even talking. I guess the ideal sounds too perfect because he tells me that it sounds like a music video, and half laughs but in a way that I'm sure is meant to be sympathetic, but I scowl and try to make it look like I'm pretending not to be hurt – it makes him apologize for making things sound trivial, even though I actually think that it makes the whole thing seem a lot more romantic and unique and above and outside the every day.

I tell him that my boyfriend and I ended up kissing again, this time so hard that our teeth crashed together and I bit the inside of my mouth. I got his spit all inside my cheeks and the faint stubble on his chin irritated my own sweaty face in this completely mind blowing way.

I say that we ended up back at my place – and I improvise like someone from this noise band I went to see last week – adding that that I got evicted from the same place after my boyfriend died and I had a nervous breakdown.

I've always had this fantasy of two people meeting and going back home to fuck, but not actually having sex: I've always imagined them standing at opposite ends of a room, both masturbating and looking at the other – so it was more like their minds were ass fucking rather than the roles that their bodies usually called predictable ownership on. I tell him that that's what happened the night of the concert, when my boyfriend and I first got back to my place. But after we came at exactly the same moment we ended up fucking anyway. We were overpowered. It felt like a choice made for us that we didn't have any sway over.

I tell him that the fucking was really heavy. I tell him that it was the sort of sex where secrets are shared between two people and that when it was over we both knew so much about each other.

There are certain things that make me feel these weird emotions that I can't describe, like how I feel driving into a city at night. If people don't understand what I mean by that then that's fine. It just means that they're a different type of person to me. Driving into a city at night, the smell of burning, boys in grey t-shirts, the sound of skateboards, putting my hand at the base of someone's back, the sound of footsteps on a hotel floor.

Talking about my imaginary dead boyfriend legitimizes a lot of stuff for me. I'm able to talk about things that if I was just being honest and relating things to myself I'd never ever even get near.

If I say that lies are a really helpful thing, you have to realize that I don't mean it in a malicious way. Lies can be pure, too.

I talk about the time that we both ended up meeting this seventeen year old BMX rider outside some lame punk gig, how we both took him home and fucked him for the first time. He was stoned and high and barely able to know what was happening but he was still somehow into it and spent the whole next day with us, looking at coffee table books of nude boys that looked just like him, before he headed off and we never saw him again properly except a couple of times in the local record shop where we'd swap these knowing grins and think about how sore our respective dicks felt for next few days after our threesome.

When I tell people about that kind of thing I feel like it denotes a certain freedom and power that I've been associated with that most people don't get to actually experience. I want people to know that I've been to places that they've never been and they'll never go. Sometimes because I've told so many lies I even start to believe this stuff myself.

He asks me more about the sex. He's masturbating while I tell him about my imaginary dead boyfriend.

I'm mentally trying to make a list of all the things that are making me feel like I should kill myself. I'm thinking about them, trying to narrow them down. I try to think about the things that my fictional boyfriend would have been driven into desperation by. With him – I don't know – how could I even begin to get my head around that stuff?

The night that my boyfriend killed himself gets changed around quite a bit, while I'm trying to explain. The guy listening doesn't care because he's close to cumming, and keeps asking for details of my dead boyfriend's body: skinny, I say, smooth I say – people need so few details when their own sexual projections are so huge that they can outweigh and overshadow the real life impetus that has triggered the projection; it's like an illusion.

I was late back through no fault of my own. If I'd been back just an hour earlier then I might have been able to save him. The implication is pretty heart-breaking – I think I might be able to see tears form in his eyes but it could be they're glazing over because he's as gone as me and I guess he's already lost somewhere other than where I want him to be. I tag on that I'd forgotten to take my phone out with me – when I checked it later there were thirteen missed calls all from him. I tell him that my boyfriend and I had had an argument over something that I don't disclose to him, probably for fear of accidentally cross wiring or miss stitching the intricate weave of sympathy that I've been threading for so long. At the end of the argument my boyfriend disappeared into another room and I fell asleep in tears, exhausted. I awoke to silence. There are a few other variations that I'm bored of falsely remembering. Sometimes I have dreams made out of these 'memories'. I've told this lie a few times over now.

"How big was his dick?"

I stop talking and walk back into the club. I think about this image of screwed up balls of aborted suicide notes that fill a waste paper bin in the corner of a bedroom. If only I can get somewhere near the note that I mythologize so much to people who are forced out of good will to believe me; but I give up. It's like trying to imagine

63

a colour that I've never seen before.

It's getting late. There's only so much you can do in a day to make yourself feel part of it.

26

I look up the details of the next Cum Worship event. On the barebacking websites, it's talked about like it's the next Wrestlemania. People post comments like they're trash talking before a fight. The language is combative but instead of talking themselves up, the guys who are sexually passive talk themselves down. They take pride in talking about just how passive, how submissive and how subservient they can be. They call themselves lowly. They call themselves worthless. They talk about tops as the givers of life and death. Cum is their oxygen. They talk about barebacking like it's some kind of undisputable truth. It's their way of knowing something, their way of knowing everything, and that without it they are nothing. It seems to be an admission of something, but I don't know what. It makes me scared and kind of nervous and sick too, but I'm also acutely aware of how hard my dick gets and how fast when I'm voyeuristically taking in the online representation of the world that they claim to be a part of. The only truth I've ever understood is confusion – that's the only constant and only certainty that I've ever been able to completely grasp and relate to.

:Hi everyone. I'm a poz'd up little piggy who is thinking or dreaming of cum twenty-four hours a day, three-hundred-and-sixty-five days a year. Even Christmas day is a let-down for me if I don't get some seed! I'll be attending the next Cum Worship event and I'll be at the service of ANYONE who wants to continue my breeding. Looking for HIV positive tops, masters, daddies, sickos, perverts, rapists – ANYONE – to feed their seed into my hole. My job is to serve you, whoever you are, regardless of age, race, looks. A true pig has NO SAY in what ANYONE does to them.

:Ditto what that pig said!

:Hi guys. I'm looking for some specific kind of porn and guessed that if there's anywhere online that would have it, then this would be the place. I'm hoping to find some internal cum shots. I want any images of videos of the cum actually entering the other guy. I don't want to see a top pulling out. I want — like an X-Ray of something, the cum going inside someone. I don't want to see cum wasted, like when the top pulls out and cums on the bottom's face, ass, body. It's waste — the cum needs to go INSIDE.

:OK. So after bug chasing for about a year, last night I finally got tested positive. It's a moment that I don't think I can put into words. I'll try anyway and this seems to be the place to do it. They were running a mobile free testing clinic at the sex club/sauna that I go to regularly. I figured that I should do it because I haven't for a while, and I've been taking as many loads as possible and have been trying to be the most promiscuous person that I can be. A quick bit about me: I'm 19, slim, no body hair, told cute, I guess what you would call a twink although I kind of feel like I want to cringe when I say that myself. But for ease of explanation I guess it makes sense and if you saw me then you would probably agree. I took the finger prick test. The nurse told me that it would take about twenty minutes so I told them I was going to go for a quick cigarette and then come back. I actually just went back into the club and jumped in the sling, and had a guy breed me bareback. When I was back talking to the nurse, I could feel the cum running down my leg. They said that "unfortunately the test showed up some HIV" in my blood. They said I have to book a hospital appointment because they aren't allowed to officially confirm it for some reason, but that I for all intents and purposes I was now HIV positive and that I would receive full support. I wasn't sure what to think last night and I'm still not one hundred per cent sure now. There was this dread but also this relief — I mean — I've got nothing to be scared of anymore, right? I've got what I've chased for so long. I've faced my fears and got things out of the way, right? I guess I wanted to post on here because I know that no one will judge and I guess that pretty much everyone else on here has got it, right? I can't talk to my friends or family or colleagues because there's no way that they're gonna understand this shit. I don't even understand it myself. I just know that at the moment I'm on this weird high, and

I feel like an angel that just got his wings.

:Welcome to the club, baby!

:Anyone up for really taboo chat? Private message me if you are.

I notice that my whole body has changed. I'm upright, tense, while
I'm reading this stuff. I don't know what I should be thinking and
I don't think I actually am thinking much. There's a reaction but I
couldn't tell you what it was. I click on the profile of the person who
wants the "really taboo chat". It's hard to work out what he would
want to talk privately about on a forum where people are talking
about trying to catch HIV.

****Guest has entered Private Chat.
****Poz4life has entered Private Chat
Guest: Hi.
Poz4life: Hi.
Guest: So what do you want to talk about.
Poz4life: Real taboo stuff – no limits, fucked up, anything goes. You?
Guest: Same. Anything. Whatever you want.
*Poz4life: Bareback, cum worship, rough sex, K9, rape, torture, real nasty, sicko
cunt here. What's your worst fantasy?*
Guest: I don't know. Yours?
*Poz4life: Full blown AIDS. I want to be fucked by a skeletal dying man. Sores
weeping all over me. Acid cum being shot inside me. Scabs scraping off on me. I
want to feel as close to death as I can, sending my virus into overdrive.*

****Guest has left Private Chat.

I'm shaking. My body has seized up over my laptop.

27

Whatever though ... the internet is just a fog that won't clear.

28

- A gif of a spooky looking house, which keeps illuminating every time that lightning strikes.
- A gif of an anime girl standing in some shadows near a window in a white room. Every couple of seconds a light flickers on and her facial expression changes to fear.
- A gif of a computer-drawn ghost, with black hair hanging down and covering its face, reaching out from inside a television.
- A gif of a green puppet frog repeatedly jumping onto a television show host's neck.
- A gif from an old horror film in black in white, with the devil stirring a cauldron over and over again.
- A gif that shows the evolution of humans – a monkey is walking, it turns into an ape walking more upright, it turns into a Neanderthal, it turns into a human, it turns into a zombie. The zombie turns around kills the human and runs back from where it came.
- A gif of a dog snarling.
- A gif of a man in a ski mask, holding a chainsaw, chasing people through some woods.
- A gif of a practical joke where a man is being interviewed and someone in a scary Halloween mask jumps out of a wheelie-bin behind him. The man being interviewed instinctively turns and punches the masked person in the face, knocking them back into the bin and effectively spoiling the practical joke's intentions.
- A gif of a woman being stabbed in the shower.
- A gif of a skeleton dancing.
- A gif of a cartoon bat dancing.
- A gif of a pumpkin dancing.

— A gif of someone wearing Black Metal style corpse paint, screaming.
— A gif of insects moving in and out of the eye sockets of a fake/prosthetic/prop head.
— A gif of a zombie, covered in blood and dirt jumping out from a muddy puddle.
— A gif from an old horror film or someone pulling on ripped out tendons, making the fingers of a hand move.
— A gif of an animated skeleton in a suit punching the air in frustration.
— A gif of a nurse falling towards a superimposed background that is presumably supposed to look like Hell.
— A gif of some grainy old footage of a skeleton, with the words GHOSTS WILL WALK AND TALK, floating on top of the image.
— A gif from what looks like an old horror movie trailer, with the words IT CAME WITHOUT WARNING flashing back and forth.

29

Anonymous: *How's the escape plan coming along?*
Dreamlifeofacutter: *Almost there.*

30

*My friends have the best intentions. They'll kinda hate me when they read this.
Some of them anyway. I hope that passes. I guess it won't matter too much to me
if it doesn't — not in a bad way; that's just me being … realistic? They know
what sorts of thing that I'd want to happen. They know the sorts of things that
I think would be crass or not my style or whatever. Not that this is a big plan or
anything. We've just talked about this stuff. I think they know — maybe we were
all too stoned. The important stuff in life is the easiest stuff to forget. I have
to have faith in people now — that's not meant to sound religious. People just
have to believe in themselves I think, but like I say, for me that's another thing
that I guess will just disappear into the air or something. I've written a couple
of lists. They're in the inlay of a punk rock album that I pretended meant a
lot more to me than it did, which made me feel sorta dumb only not as dumb
as I would have felt if people didn't believe that I understood or got it or felt
the same religious experience that they used to say that they got when they heard
the distortion and the shouting and thought about skateboards and fucking and
politics and whatever else was meant to important — the nothingness, I think. I
think I always felt that the nothingness was vague, but if I didn't pretend that
that nothingness meant something big; well … More air. Dust. Haha — yeah,
let's say dust. One of the lists is full of passwords: they can get into all my social
networking sites — even the fake ones that I set up to spy on people that I was
too scared to talk to, they can shut those down for me or put out a bulletin saying
what had happened to me, or maybe just turn the pages into memorials that can
float in cyberspace until the internet is just one big digital graveyard of people
who died, got bored, or both. I wonder if it's possible to haunt the internet.
I'm hoping that by now someone will have got the password for my laptop and
deleted all the pornography and nude pictures that I've sent out to people that
I've met online. I need to stop my parents from ever seeing that stuff — it just
wouldn't be in their best interests or in the interests of the memory that I'm trying
to leave traces of. All this is because I'm impatient: I don't want to have to wait*

for things to get better, because people have been telling me about that for so long that I can't believe that it's true anymore. I've never met anyone that's happy in the way that I'm supposed to believe it's meant to be. I've never seen one couple that's happy together — I mean like totally happy. I'm convinced that my parents are only together because it would be more bother to not be. None of my friends treat the people that they're with properly, and my own pathetic attempts at being with people always fuck up because I'm too jealous, paranoid and insecure to even admit half of the things that I'd like to let them know. It's too late to change things and too early to warrant waiting around to sort stuff out. People would probably blame that sort of stuff on Youtube if I said it out loud; people like to simplify others so they can complicate themselves. I think I meant adults when I wrote that, but my friends like to feel complicated too. We've got this whole thing about being smart. I'm pretty sure that we're smarter than most of the other fifteen year olds that we know, but there's still this competition … we're not trying to make each other look bad though, so I guess that puts us one up on our parents. My parents start nodding before I've even finished a sentence. My dad says "I know" or "yeah" when I try to tell him something, like he knew it already, or sometimes he tries to interrupt, but when I carry on talking he just waits till I've finished and completes what he had already decided to say. There's a big difference between hearing things and listening to things, and he just doesn't get it. My friends have weird ways of describing certain situations. I can't really predict how they'll take this. I don't know. It depends how stoned they are. A couple of them, I know they'll feel really bad, but it isn't like I want them too, which is why I'd better write this next bit: this is so not your fault, I promise you that. And I wouldn't say things unless I meant them — I probably have in the past, but not this time, because this is the first time that I'm trying to be one hundred percent honest (and just for the record — it's fucking hard!!! Even just being honest with myself feels like I'm trying to catch water in a net). They'll call this monumental. Maybe they won't call it anything. I'm mainly hoping that if they hate me then it won't last forever because that would be unfair on them, and doubly so because I wouldn't even have to live with the guilt. I guess that's why I'm going to leave certain secrets exactly how they are as well, because it wouldn't be me who would have to sort the pieces out when things started to feel broken. Even stuff about fucking — I almost wanted to write a list of who had given the best oral, or something dumb like that, until I realized what an idiot it would make sound. I also wanted to make a list of the nicest and the most important things that people have ever said to me. In some ways I thought that that list would be a better idea than the oral sex list but it would still come down to the same thing, with both of the lists, certain people would end up wishing that they'd done more. I worked out that it's for the best if I just leave memories just as they are right now. Memories are totally untrustworthy anyways, and me doing what I'm going to do as soon as I finish writing this might change everyone's memory anyway — like the last time we got stoned near the lake in the park — maybe that would stop feeling like boredom and whatever else it feels like now and turn into ... the last supper? I'm laughing because I'm thinking of what we'd all look like on a painting like that. It'd probably look really cool ... we could always Photoshop it or something. I wonder if people can Photoshop death. Maybe that's what has always happened. It's just easier for us to retouch corpses if they're online. I think I might be trying to say that every photograph is death. What would that make my friends and me? Morticians? I think we must know death pretty well. We've put so much of a slant on pictures of us that we've removed pretty much any life we had in the first place and replaced it with something else. I think I read that it's called the parallax — but I lost interest pretty quick. But basically it's all about there being a gap between what we want the photographs to be and what they actually are. Maybe it just means that we're failures. I'm probably not even finishing this properly. But thinking about my friends makes it seem a lot more — I was going to say real and then I realized how stupid that sounds. If you don't know what I mean by that then fuck you. You'll never understand and I'll never get to explain it to you because this is it. If you think that this is for you then it is and if you're not convinced that it is but wish it wasn't then pretend that it isn't because that's cool too. Fuck it. I'm sorry. I'm sorry for all of this.

31

:I can't do this anymore. A sad face.

32

The warmth hits me as I walk into the room. It sounds like the bass is moving from one wall to another, like the music is shifting as a mass, ricocheting around the club, sound spreading itself thickly across every corner, leaving traces, invisible graffiti messages and codes that no one will ever read, but that everyone understands. The room is dizzy. The room is moving. Men are fucking, everywhere. Someone touches my back as I order a drink. When I turn around, they're gone. It's like a ghost, or a cumulative spirit. I feel sick and I feel alive. Bodies gather around each other, immerse, meld and then scatter. It's like looking at organisms through a microscope. Everything is in flux all of the time and nothing is fixed and no one notices, which is how the illusion works, I guess. I don't know anything for sure. I move further into the darkroom. Nothing matters. I'm feeling my way through the darkness. I'm sculpting shadows into jewels. I'm in their arms.

THE END

Lightning Source UK Ltd.
Milton Keynes UK
UKHW020642310522
403779UK00010B/735